Intrigued

A Journey

A
Novella
By

Bonny Mayorga

Published by Bonny Mayorga

'INTRIGUED A Journey'

Copyright © Bonny Mayorga 2015

First publication 2015

Published by Bonny Mayorga

Email: bonnymayorga@gmail.com

Original illustrations/ Photographs by Image Fusion.

URL: http://www.image-fusion.co.uk

Intrigued A Journey

Author: Bonny Mayorga

Editor: Jose Mayorga

ISBN 978-0-9934697-1-8

Paperback Edition

Acknowledgements

I would like to express appreciation to my wonderful husband for all the support he has provided me during this process of writing my book.

Many thanks to image fusion having created the magnificent illustrations and book cover to ensure my book looks as good as it reads.

To Aga.
Enjoy the Journey.
Love Bonny X

3

Synopsis

Life for most is confusing, however for Misha it was much more than she could handle. From one day to the next she didn't know if she was living life or if life was controlling her.

Misha believes she can travel. Her husband believes it's an illness. She struggles with everything thrown at her, she deals with it the only way she can by deviating from her life.

Her husband is supportive. Is he the only one that knows what's going on?

Or is Misha right, can she travel?
What you choose to believe is up to you.

Why don't you travel on this journey with Misha and remember to keep an open mind in this mystery
Are you intrigued?

Contents

Courtesy of Image Fusion

Chapter 1
The Introduction

As my arm flopped over the edge of the bed, the pure guilt trickled down my cheeks. I was not proud of myself at all, there is no excuse for it. Looking up at the ceiling with my teary glazed eyes, wishing I had gone straight home. The quietness in the room was almost unbearable.

There was so much to do, it was all running through my head like a non-stop train. As I turned over, I felt his fingers run through my hair as I scrunched my eyes close, hoping he hadn't realised I was awake. I was cringing on the inside. I just wanted to slip away. Obviously it was too late now.

His warm fingers ran down through my scalp down the back of my neck and slickly down my arm, he grabbed my hand and turned me on my back. He threw his legs over my groin with his weight overpowering my scrawny body, he kissed my neck so gently with his marshmallow lips, it made me tingle, using his tongue to make circular motions on my breast, he took my nipple through his teeth, while his right hand slipped into my underwear, you could hear the tear of the cotton as he pulled them down my silky legs.

Then the vibrations of my phone stopped him in his motions.

"Not again" he muttered to himself, but I heard him, off course, with my extra sensory hearing (like most women).

He slipped out of the bed with a sigh, covered my bare skin, he slammed the bathroom door behind him but it bounced open, that damn door needed fixing. I could hear him turn the shower on.

I lay there for a moment, again staring at the ceiling, I pulled my underwear back up my legs and sat on the end of the bed and huddled my head in my hands. I picked up my jeans from the floor and just as I pulled out my phone.

"Honey! Can you pass me the towel? It's on the end of the bed".

I thought to myself, that was a bloody quick shower. I placed my arm round the door with the towel and he pulled me in.

"Now I have you" he said in his husky voice. He loved to play around with me.

I dropped the phone behind me as he pushed me against the shower glass with his left fingers intertwined with mine and his right hand pulling down my underwear. His wet body pressed against mine, I felt like I couldn't breathe, not in panic but in fact excitement. The light went out.

Well actually it was my candle as it flickered and blew out, I finally came back up for air, in fact I was dreaming. I fell asleep in the bath, the wine glass dropped through my fingers as my arm hung over the bath edge. I had sunk under the water for moments but what felt like hours.

Let me tell you a bit about myself;

My name is Misha. I am in my early thirty's' (I'm not one for ever being honest about my age). I would like to think of myself as voluptuous and sassy, with bottom length, rich cranberry red, tight curly locks. I try to dress to impress, but also to make me feel sensual.

My life is a rollercoaster, the only thing that keeps me alive is my dreams, most people don't remember them, however to me they are so vivid and emotional they seem real, I feel in control. I sometimes cannot differentiate between the two worlds. There is much more to this than meets the eye, you will find out soon enough! I seem to get lost in random, or I should say unexplainable moments.

Most people dream about falling, the lack of control in their life, for some reason mine is sexual trying to gain that control where I don't find this in my reality. The water seems to calm and relax me and bring me back to reality, this is why I love taking baths so often. However today I could feel that I was starting to lose some of that control.

I believe there is a hidden message in my dreams, I am still yet to interpret this. I seem to be addicted and obsessed with what I don't possess.

No glass to sip my wine! Instead I picked up the wine bottle from next to the bath and took a swig of it from the bottle neck. I am not going to lie to you, but I have struggled a lot with life, as do most people, its how you make it to the other side. I am not quite there yet, which you can tell from the almost healed, slashes on my wrists and thighs. Somethings are too painful to talk about, even more to think about on a daily basis; these dreams help me block things out.

"Baby, are you okay in there, I heard something smash?".

"Yes, Honey, sorry, I dropped the wine glass, again! I nodded off in the bath".

My husband came into the bathroom (I always leave the door unlocked) he kindly brushed the glass and handed me another and then re-lit my candle, followed by a kiss on my forehead then a slip of his hand under the water to fondle my nipples (always made me giggle).

I seem to do this on a regular basis, break things that is. He always seems to be there to pick up the pieces.

"You relax my love" closing the door behind him and a cheeky wink.

My Husband;

When I first set my eyes on him, there was some coyness between us and a sensation of comfort and trust instantaneously. A feeling which is indescribable, difficult to place in to words. Not just with his strapping physique, but I actually developed feelings for him immediately. My close friend set us up on a date (I in fact thought I was meeting her for drinks, I was actually glad it wasn't her I met that night). I don't refer to him as babe like most people or even use his name, husband feels comforting, knowing that I'm his wife, makes me feel a sense of pride.

The night we met, he gave me that tingly exiting feeling that made me crave him when we were not together. When we were together, that rush of pleasure made me feel ecstasy, like a drug. His warm hugs and long arms enthralled round me, gazing up at him, I felt I was at home. I felt the jigsaw finally come together.

He smelt sweet like candy, even if I closed my eyes and he walked pass me or through a room full of people, I would recognise his scent and know he was there. He made me laugh so much, the way he used his personality to win me over. He is the kindest, most selfless person I think I would ever know. He makes me his priority and always puts me ahead of himself. (I do feel quite a selfish person when I am with him).

A tall 6'4, rugged, but not scruffy look, a perky bum and a sweet scent. A man who knows how to give a girl a good time. I mean who would say no to that.

My thoughts staggering into a heady state of forgetfulness, as the wine trickles down my throat, there is a patter of rain against the window with a sudden downpour. Before I knew it, I nodded off and I was back in the shower.

He gathered me in his arms, I lifted my head up against the glass. These are crazy moments where desires seek to deceive me. Am I unfaithful? Is it wrong to want these moments to be real, to just separate myself from the real world, I do not want to betray myself or my husband.

He continued to pull down my underwear, down my wet body, he caressed me all over with his hands and lips. He placed his hands under my body to lift me up on his already erect penis, within a blink he was already inside me. Once he came, he turned around with his back to me and continued to shower.

I stepped out and wrapped myself in my silk nightgown hung on the hook behind the door, as I slammed the door behind me, it actually shut for a change.

Then the husband shouted "I'm going now, see you tomorrow, love you, mwah" and then the door slammed behind him. Back to reality, and yet again I dropped the wine glass. So I carefully stepped out my bath and walked around the shattered pieces.

Sometimes he works away and we have to spend a few days apart, maybe this is where my loneliness began, I just yearn attention. I know it's no excuse.

Then the doorbell chimed. I ran downstairs, opened the door, and kissed his lips before pulling him in with my long well-groomed nails, by the cuff of his shirt.

The Affair;

Marc, is the name of my sordid affair.

I know, I am a terrible person. But as I began to lose control of my life, he was the only thing that I felt I had control over. I was drawn to him with familiar traits to my husband, you know that rugged look, and he has a similar scent which drew me in straight away. He's single, no ties and knows how to give me a buzz.

There was a sense of excitement, thrill and maybe a bit of the danger too. This is real, my dreams are just fantasy. These are the traits my husband and I had over the years which had slowly disappeared.

Obviously I did not set out to have an affair, it just happened. He filled a void that I had lost with my husband, over the years we slowly grew apart, I don't think I will ever know why or how to fix it. He was my distraction, or you could say escapism!

Courtesy of Image Fusion

17

Chapter 2
The Beginning

"That was close, he just left, you should have waited a few more minutes", I said.

"A few less minutes with you, every minute counts. It's raining so much out there Misha, I need to get out of these wet clothes".

Now...... doesn't he have a way with words?

As he ran in and stood on the first step of the staircase dripping, staring at me with his smouldering eyes. I pulled him back. He knows the house like it's his own. I ripped the shirt off his chest, the buttons popped off and dropped to the mahogany wooden floor. I provocatively untied the rope of my silk nightgown and it slipped to the floor.

"I will warm you up" I said in my seductive voice. I undid the button to his trousers, unzipped them, turned around and sat on the 3rd step like a confident 20 year old, that I'm not! I spread my legs wide pulled him towards my face and whispered, "Make love to me, until I scream".

He began by rubbing his right hand against my already wet vagina, up and down, my clit began to widen. He then lowered his already unzipped trousers and began running his hard penis against my vagina, slowly entering, he placed his muscular body against my breasts, making slow motions, empowering me with his weight, he placed his arms around my waist, embracing my body against his, I gasped in and out deeply, tilted my head back before screeching in a high tone with delight.

We never needed many words to express our feelings, clearly!

We lay there a few moments; trust me it was not as uncomfortable as you are imagining on the stairs, not when you are in the moment. He then placed his hands under my buttocks for a quick feel before he gathered me in his arms and slowly took me upstairs to the bedroom, where I just lay in his arms until the morning.

I woke up to the sun rays peering through the slighted open curtains, the birds tweeting, the smell of freshly ground coffee and a pain au chocolat….oh and an empty side of the bed. I heard the toilet flush, as I sat up to make myself comfortable, the husband came out of the bathroom.

"Morning sweetheart, did you sleep well? My trip got cancelled so I drove all night to make it back in time to see your beautiful morning face".

With a confused look on my face, when did Marc leave? I asked myself.

He had a way with words, he does make my heart flutter and my knees go weak (if I was standing for sure) and he knows how to make me feel special. At this point I should be feeling guilty that I am having an affair. Not being able to look into my husband's eyes, but no, that would be a lie. I felt a rush, an exhilaration and the fact that I could have got caught; I wouldn't have minded about the consequences. You could say I have a passionate infatuation or attachment with Marc.

"Come on baby, you need to get ready or you'll be late".

I forget to mention I see a Holistic Counsellor, some of you may think I have issues. Well don't we all? I just need to see someone who understands me.

Holistic Counsellor;

Or as I refer to as 'My Counsellor'. This type of counselling isn't just about me talking, and the counsellor listening. Holistic counselling helps me feel peace and optimism. My counsellor is also trained in psychotherapy, who also meditates a lot. This was the beginning of my journey. Before going, I did feel sceptical so I researched online and in one sentence it explained Holistic Counselling, which made me feel more comfortable.

Holistic Counselling

'An alternative form of psychotherapy that focuses on the whole person; mind, body and spirit and health. The goal is growth of the whole person'. Mosby's Medical Dictionary.

I just need to focus on that goal, whatever it may be (still figuring this out).

So as well as being a possible suicide patient (I won't lie I have tried a few times, and obviously failed), I am a cheat, a liar and possibly mentally unstable. Can it get any worse? And I haven't even been married a year yet!

So many thoughts are running through my head as I'm getting ready, still with the stench of sex on my body, (no time for a shower, to wash away my sins) my husband watching me like I'm falling to pieces, any wonder I'm deviating from my life.

I just can't escape!

Keep calm, I say to myself in my head, 1,2,3,4, 5 and breathe, don't show the cracks. Let's paint over them with an inch of make-up, which always makes me feel so much better.

After painting on my face for the day, I passingly kissed the husband goodbye, made my way to the car and sat in the driver's seat. (We have stopped saying I love you to each other).

Whilst I turned on the engine I dialled Marc's number. It just kept ringing and ringing there was no answer. Did he ever pick up his phone? No! I quickly typed him a text.

When did u sneak out?
He's back already.
Had a gr8 nite.
C u L8r LU X

I then made my way to the counsellor's office.

My counsellor, hmmm... where do I start? I knocked on her door. (That's a good start).

"Come in" she shouted in her stern tone.

I had interrupted her, there she is in the Buddhist pose, hands in the Namaste position, humming...

"Om.. Om.. Om.. Om.."

With her fitted leggings, accentuating her tight bottom and bright pink sports top.

She was as still and as calm as a fly on the wall, I just wanted to flick her! (I am sure you would too).

Lana, my counsellor, long golden wavy hair, the tiniest nose stud glaring at me from the door. Her office, wasn't the typical set up with a table, chair and chez lounge.

"Om...." as she exhaled.

"Make yourself comfortable".

I slipped off my shoes outside the office before I entered and slowly shut the door behind me. You may not believe me know, but you will find out that what goes on in the room, stays in the room.

I knelt down to make myself comfy between the silky cushions and white fluffy rug on the floor. So basically her office was empty, it was just Lana, myself and these cushions. Lana's moto is *an empty space, opens up opportunities to a clearer mind and a walkable path.'* Then she began, the session in her sturdy Buddhist pose.

We have had many sessions, they all start pretty much the same, well apart from Lana beginning in a different pose. Even though I think I could probably do this without her, she always says we should go through the motions together, as support if something goes wrong. You will realise why soon enough.

"Lie down and close your eyes, place your arms down the side of your body and clear your mind…. Ommmmmmm, and slowly breathe out through your feet, let the tension seep from the top of your body and escape out at the bottom of your toes and release" (when we first started these sessions, I couldn't help but giggle to myself).

I continued with my deep breathing, it felt like the room filled up with steam and within moments I felt as if my soul had departed my shell of a body. As I gradually opened my eyes, I was stood in the centre of Lana's boxed office.

I looked up as the light began to flicker, I looked back down I could see a grey shadow of Lana's Buddhist pose. Go on do it, I thought it would be funny to try and push her over but as I tried to push, I just fell over. Then the light went out.

I was laying on the floor, I seemed to be unconscious. Can you believe it from falling over!

Chapter 3
Travel the Distance

"Misha, Misha… can you hear me" I could hear Lana faintly shouting at me.

I was shaking vigorously for a few moments. Then it stopped.

This is no ordinary counselling as you can tell, well I am no ordinary person and you are probably wondering what's happening and why I am seeing what you may think is an unconventional Counsellor!.

Well… I seem to be able to travel from reality to different points in time, i.e. my imagination (or you may think I just simply have psychological issues!) In this case my imagination and I don't seem to differentiate between what is real and what is my imagination, it is like a deep dream, and with this I seem to have gained a dual personality. Well I am a Gemini! This is why I see a Holistic Counsellor.

One day this will land me into trouble, I am sure and that's what scares me the most, is when I don't really know if I am in control. So this is no ordinary Counsellor, you could say that we are on more or less the same wavelength.

After my vigorous shaking, I steadily picked myself back up off the floor, I turned around the room and there was a bed behind me. It was my bed, it was unmade, just as I left it this morning. I didn't understand what was going on and why I was here. So I thought I would take advantage, I crawled back into bed.

My surroundings began to gradually transform into my bedroom, this didn't seem to faze me at all. I started to nod off into a deep sleep, until I felt someone push me to the other side of the bed. I suddenly awoke, my heart was pounding with fear.

"Whose there? Hello, is anyone there?".

As I gripped the edge of the duvet close to my body. I felt uneasy, on edge, just as thoughts began to run through my mind, it was so quiet, then my husband's head popped round the corner and I jumped out of my skin.

"Morning sweetheart, did you sleep well? My trip got cancelled so I drove all night to make it back in time, to see your beautiful morning face".

What's going on, it's like Deja Vu! I paused for a few moments. Is this possible? Is my morning being re-created, maybe this is my opportunity to turn things around. There has been so much tension between me and my husband, Could I make it right?

"Come on baby, you need to get ready, or you will be late" he repeated again as he did earlier.

So I said, "Why don't you join me in bed baby? I have 10 minutes", using my finger to order him to bed, with a mischievous wink.

He came round the other side of the bed, pulled his t-shirt over his head and threw it behind him over his shoulder and crawled in under the duvet. He placed his arm under my head, pulled me close to his warm, yet slightly wet body. He just stared into my weary blue eyes, with so much love. He kissed my forehead with his gentle lips, stroking my hair.

You know what, I actually felt safe in his arms, I closed my eyes to soak up this rare moment, I cleared my mind of all the shit going on. I wanted to savour this moment forever, He is definitely my addiction, my obsession in life.

"Shall I come with you today baby? I'd like to support you and see how you are progressing".

Panic set over my already trembling, weary body.

"No! No!" I repeated.

"I will be fine, you can see how I'm doing, you can see it, can't you?"

I said with hesitation, waiting acknowledgement. I was saying it to him, but did I mean it? Am I really getting better?

"I'm almost at the end of my sessions, I don't want to go backwards".

I then tore myself away from him, while he just lay there starring at the ceiling, took a deep breath and sighed. He watched me as I paced across the room, huffing and puffing away to myself, then he exhaled.

There was the car horn resonating from outside, I ran straight to the window, it was Marc.

"Who is it baby?" As he sat up in bed.

"It's my taxi, I didn't feel like driving today, I'm meeting the girls later for drinks too".

I was definitely not meeting the girls for drinks. As I was walking out the bedroom, the husband got out of bed and grabbed my hand, as I turned, he looked at me, he really looked at me in the eyes, like he wanted to say something. Before he had chance to get out his first word, I interrupted him.

"I really have to go". I pecked him on the cheek and left the room.

I made a swift exit and ran straight to the car, I jumped into the passenger seat, turned to look at Marc, kissed him on his left cheek as he revved his engine and sped off. As he did I looked back at the house, I saw the curtains twitching from the bedroom. Damn that was close!

Did he catch a glimpse of Marc?

I loved to live on the edge, I always have an urge to do something exhilarating.

"What are we doing today baby?" I said in such a loving tone.

"Whatever you wish my love" as he took his eyes off the road to gaze into mine. I pushed my hand against his cheek to turn back at the road.

"Concentrate, on where you are going....... I know, lets' go to the lake, it will be fun!".

"But you can't swim" he Shakely said, moving his head side to side. As much as the water calms me when I'm having a bath, it scares me to death when I can't feel the floor, where it makes me feel safe and grounded.

"I will be fine, I will hold on to you". He knows how stubborn I am. There's no tactic he could use to even think of changing my mind.

We got to the lake, even before he had stopped the car, I jumped straight out and left the door open behind me. You could hear the crunch of him pulling up the handbrake echo behind me as I ran to the water's edge, pulling off my shoes behind me.

As I got to the edge I suddenly halted. I felt a sense of ecstasy, buzz through me like a current of electricity, yet a little uncertainty and hesitation of getting into the water. I closed my eyes and simply inhaled the fresh air and then exhaled. I could hear rustling through the grass behind me.

I turned my head over my right shoulder to see Marc stood behind me. I then dipped my right toes into the water. It made me shudder for a moment at the icy temperature. But that won't stop me!

"Are you sure?" he said.

I didn't say anything. I continued to drop my dress to the freshly cut grass still keeping my underwear on, grabbed his hand before he had even pulled his shirt off and I jumped in and took him with me. I went under for a few moments. Panic had begun to sink in.

Before I could even think, Marc grabbed me by the waist and pulled me to the surface, my pristine hair now soaked from root to tip, this was not a sexy moment, as I tried to flick my head to the left hoping my hair would return to its normal self!.

"There you are!" as he gripped me tightly. I enthralled my hands round his neck. I was gripped to him so harshly that my nails had broken his skin. But he did not whimper with any pain. He just lifted the hair away from my face and placed it neatly behind my ears.

We just gazed at each other, there was no need for us to exchange conversation.

We relished the moment, he kissed me so romantically.

His hands unhooked my bra (under water, what a skill I must say!) and then his fingers began to patter below my waist, he fondled my bottom squeezing each cheek simultaneously. I mean who wouldn't have a fondle in an excluded, peaceful lake with no prying eyes. I remember looking up at the blue sky with the clouds parting into random shapes.

The way he held on to me, I began to feel more and more relaxed, my tense body began to feel at ease. I lowered my arms from his neck down to hold his hands as I felt more comfortable. We circled around in the water for a while and then just gradually seemed to float towards the centre of the lake, you could hear the ripples of the water as they fluttered in crimped motions and nothing else.

All of a sudden he let go of me. I didn't know if he was playing around with me or if it was real. Then I began to feel anxious, my heart was pounding against my chest wall.

"Wwwwhhat are you doing" I bellowed at him.

"You will be fine, I'm here" he said amused, paddling backwards away from me, leaving my hands, with a very relaxed expression on his face. I was not finding this amusing.

I began treading the water, kicking my legs. My breathing was rapidly increasing in angst. I was worn out trying to stay afloat, for a moment I went under. Marc swam towards me and tried to grab my hand and as I reached out for him, I just about touched his fingers but could not get the grip.

Before I knew it I was completely under the water. I opened my eyes under trying to locate him, splashing, trying to call out for help. A hand was reaching out for me, I could see the shadow of the fingers, but couldn't get a grip. It was disappearing further and further away.

I could hear my name being echoed and bubbles under the surface.

"Misha, Misha, can you hear me? I'm here, just reach out, I've got you". I could hear this repeatedly, but couldn't see anyone or anything.

Then suddenly everything went a shady black, and it was peaceful. I felt trapped in my body but could not find the surface. I tried to scream but there was no sound echoing from my mouth.

After a few moments, which felt like a lifetime. I fought for some air, I struggled to get back to the surface and then I came round in Lana's office with just my underwear on. I was struggling to breathe, I began coughing up water from the lake. How is this possible? I thought to myself.

Lana was holding onto my wrist mumbling something to me, I could see her mouth moving, but couldn't hear anything that she was saying. She had even got out of her Buddhist pose to flap her arms at me. (That is rare for her to come out of position) She did look slightly freaked out. I actually think it was her that pulled me out from under the water.

How is this possible?

When I eventually came back to my senses and sat up, Lana had wrapped a towel round me and handed me a hot ginger and lemon water.

"What the hell, I told you what you fear in this life, any other life will affect you the same, it's no different!"

Again she continued with the lecture.

"We need to get you checked out at the hospital, we have discussed this so many times, you know if you get in too deep, you can get yourself in trouble, and next time I might not be able to pull you out, I might not be there".
She said in her irritating, patronizing tone, which sometimes got under my skin, even knowing that she is right. All I hear is bla bla bla!

She helped me off the floor and ushered me out the door, straight into her car.

"I'm not taking any risks, Misha, you don't look so good".

Chapter 4
A Gift

Not far from the hospital, a few dozen sneezes later and light headiness, all the energy was zapped out of me. She started again!

"I think we should call your husband sweaty, we have to tell him this is serious now" Lana said, turning to look at my vacant face for a response.

"No, don't! You know he won't understand what's going on, how will I explain all this to him? I'm still figuring this out myself, does he really need to ever know?"

We sat in the emergency department for hours, still coughing and now shivering. We finally got in to see someone.

I lay there on the bed, a nurse came in and took my blood pressure.

"Are you feeling light headed" the nurse asked.

"No, why? Should I?" I responded.

"Well, your BP is abnormally low, to a point where by now you should have at least passed out" the nurse hesitated a few moments, with a bemused look on her face.

"We will just monitor you until the doctor comes, but please let me know if you feel any worse, in the meantime I am going to send your bloods off straight away".

If only she knew how I really felt! I almost nodded off and then Lana shook me.

The doctor pulled the curtain back to enter and drew it behind him.

"Well young lady, what have you been up to?" as he picked up my medical chart, flicking the pages back scanning it, nodding his head left and right. Was he really reading it? The nurse then walked in and handed the doctor a piece of paper.

"Hmmm, hmmm….. So congratulations" I looked at Lana, she looked back at me in confusion.

"Well…. you are going to be a mother, from what we can tell you are about 6 months pregnant, you better prepare yourself. Any questions, the nurse here can answer, but for now I suggest plenty of bed rest, and no more swimming, if you cannot stay afloat, we don't want anything happening to you or that little one you are protecting. I suggest a follow up with your GP".

"Congratulations" Lana said with a smile ear to ear, while she was squeezing my hand.

Tears began to trickle down my cheeks. For a moment I felt scared, I didn't know what kind of life I would be bringing this child into. If only I could take control, everything will be okay. I just have to believe this will all turn out for the best.

Then a daunting thought began to fester in my head.

Is this Marc's baby or my husband's? How could I do this, to be so reckless and not even know the father to my baby? How can I be one of these women, I felt shame overshadow me. I started to feel on edge. I closed my eyes.

"1,2,3,4,5 and breathe, breathe" again "1,2,3,4,5 and breathe".

I can't think like this, I should be enjoying this moment.

"Come on then sweaty, I will drop you off home, and you can tell that gorgeous husband of yours".

The journey home seemed to drag, I was going round and round in my head, trying to work out the dates, asking myself all these questions;

- ❖ Whose baby is it?
- ❖ What will I say to my husband, will he be happy?

- ❖ And what do I say to Marc, do I finish it before he realises I am pregnant? Does he really want all of this? Do I even need to tell him?

- ❖ Will my crazy off the track life affect this little one? (Whilst rubbing my tummy, with a big grin on my face).

I got out of the car, slammed the door behind me, breathed in and sighed out. I simply starred at the house from the bottom of the path, still with a towel wrapped round me, shivering. Then the curtain twitched and the husband ran out.

"Baby, are you okay, what happened? Why are you wet? I thought you went to your session?".

He just kept firing questions at me. I suddenly felt slightly dizzy, before I passed out and fell over he caught me and ushered me quickly back into the house. He sat me on the edge of the sofa.

"Let me get you out of these wet clothes, we don't want you catching the flu, do we?".

He began peeling my clothes off me, whilst I sat there, not even trying to help. He wrapped his nightgown round me, which always made me feel cosy, picked up my feet to lay me flat on the sofa. He then sat at the other end of the sofa with my legs in his lap and he began to massage my feet.

Then I began......

"I have something to tell you....." I muttered quietly and nervously.

"Yes, first tell me how the hell you got in this state?"

"Never mind what happened to me, please Honey don't interrupt me until I have told you".

"Tell me what?........you are worrying me".

"You better start on that spare room, we are going to have to start using it in the next 3 months…. You are going to be a dad".

He was ecstatic, he dropped my legs back on the sofa and jumped up with his arms in the air, with happy tears. He hugged me so tight and whispered in my ear.

"I love you, did I tell you I'm also so proud of you".

It dawned on me that the next 3 months were going to be tough, firstly I wasn't really looking after myself, secondly I am 6 months pregnant and I didn't even realise.

Yes I didn't have my regular monthly cycle but that has been the norm with me. There was the stress, the dieting and I suppose I am barely showing a bump, I should count myself lucky, it won't take me long to get my figure back into shape.

Plus I suppose my hormones were constantly up and down, how was I to know?

Courtesy of Image Fusion

Chapter 5
The Baby

So the baby journey began.

After finding out that we were pregnant. I realised it wasn't as easy as I thought. I had to stop drinking. The most difficult obstacle to overcome was my *'travelling'*. This I was shortly going to find out.

So after long discussions with my husband, he suggested that as I am improving from my many sessions and now that 'we' are pregnant, I should stop going to counselling, seen as I have something to focus on.

"Okay, okay I will stop going, let me just do one last session this week, then we can look forward, so we can draw a line under all of this" I said to him.

But I didn't really believe what I was saying, if anything I was hoping I would begin to believe it, the more I said it, it may actually happen. In fact I was feeling even more vulnerable now, more than ever. Can I do this? Well I hope so.

Literally days after finding out, my husband wanted to start the nursery already, I had a feeling we were going to have a boy, the husband was tempted to go for the typical blues and greens as society would accept. But as we walked into the room to discuss how to arrange everything, I had a sudden feeling of unease over my body, with shivers down my spine, a sudden cold feeling in the room. Something was not right.

I began to feel dizzy, just as the darkness was about to take over and I passed out, I started to count in my head whilst clutching on to the door firmly as to not concern the husband.

"Baby, what colours do you think we should go for? I really think we should do blue and green, I know we don't know the sex yet, but I feel sure." I was thinking in my head, it's only a few hours, why can't he wait! I suppose it's the excitement.

So yes the first scan is organised. I have to drink plenty of water, especially for the scan (as if I don't pee enough already!).

Just before we left I hadn't realised I had one hand placed on my stomach, rubbing my tummy (maybe we do it subconsciously) There were a few kicks against my stomach wall.

"Baby, quick feel, the baby's kicking and by the feel of it, a good right hook" as a hand print indent against my stomach. It was an unforgettable, exiting moment.

On the journey to the hospital the husband had made a suggestion;

"What do you think of the doctors telling myself only of the sex of the baby, that way I can complete the nursery and surprise you when I'm finished? You can relax, put your feet up, plus all them paint fumes can't be good for you or the baby".

I was slightly hesitant to say yes immediately, but I wasn't really feeling myself so I agreed.

When we got into the cubicle, the nurse asked me a few routine questions.

"So how have you been feeling generally Misha?"

"Yes, fine... we only found out a few days ago that we are having a baby".

As she was pulling the blood pressure strap up my arm, pumping away at the little squidgy thing at the bottom.

"Are you sleeping okay?".

What is this I thought to myself, is she looking at the dark puffy circles round my eyes, which looked like running mascara?

"Yes, fine".

"Well, your blood pressure seems to be quite low, do you ever feel light headed?"

"Well…. Sometimes" I replied, however this was starting to sound familiar.

"I will take some bloods just to make sure, but you could be lacking in iron. We suggest a routine check-up with your GP if you haven't already done so, then they will be able to discuss anything else that comes up in your bloods, but I am sure there is nothing to worry about".

So we had the scan, it was amazing, a 3D image, it was like the baby was physically in the room with us, all its features were so prominent. Its little nose, hands and feet. We took away a few pictures with us. The husbands face was glowing, he already looked so proud (probably because he knew the sex).

The husband vowed to the nurse that he would look after us and make sure we rest all the way up to the birth. "I'm not letting you out of my sight" he said. Then true to his word that was the first thing he did! As soon as we returned home from the hospital.

"Right now my love, you lay on this sofa and relax, watch some TV, read a book, as long as I do not see you get up, you and this baby are my number one priority" as he rubbed my stomach and lay baby books on the coffee table, baby names, and your first baby.

I was so comfy on the sofa, I picked up the baby names, flicking through, and I got to letter 'K before I knew it I had fallen asleep. Within moments I could hear the fading echo of footsteps slowly disappearing of the husband up the stairs.

As I awoke, I seemed to have made it back into the car with Marc just as I finished saying; "let's go to the lake" (this is beginning to feel familiar again, or is it? Maybe my mind is playing tricks on me.

We got to the lake, even before he stopped the car, I jumped straight out and left the door open behind me. I ran to the waters' edge, pulling off my shoes behind me. As I got to the edge I suddenly halted. However this time as I leant forward to jump in, Marc was stood behind and grabbed me round the stomach.

"There is no way you are going in there", he spun me round and grabbed me in a position to dance, and he turned on his phone in his pocket where he already had his music ready to play.

It was actually quite romantic. When the first track came to an end, he threw me out to his right, still holding my hand, to see behind me that he had laid on a picnic. How the hell did he predict I wanted to come here and have time to prepare all this! Either way I was going to enjoy it.

He had done well, he had prepared all my favourite foods and drink.

We lay on the picnic rug, he was feeding me all these lovely foods, in such a romantic serene location where you could only hear the tweeting of birds, as we laughed, revelling in one another's company. Time didn't exist when we were together.

Feeling so full always makes me sleepy, as usual I had fallen asleep with classical music humming in the background, lay over Marc as he also nodded off.

I am a light sleeper, It wasn't long until I started to hear weeping which woke me. I sat up and looked around, we were in the middle of nowhere and I couldn't see anyone. I shook my head and went to lay back down and the weeping began again.

Without trying to wake up Marc I crept up and I peered around the surroundings. Quietly I walked around for about 5 minutes I also looked behind the swaying trees, but nothing. Maybe I imagined it.

So I stood at the edge of the water to enjoy the calmness. Not even a bubble in the water. As I spun my foot round to turn, the water began to ripple which made my heart flutter, awaiting a fish to appear to the surface. It did not. Then it was calm again. All of a sudden more and more ripples running through the water.

This began to unease me as the ripples got more and more vigorous. Then from the centre of the lake the water seemed to part as the weeping got louder, I turned to look at Marc thinking he might awaken, but nothing!.

Then unexpectedly I could see some hands waving out of the slightly parted water, bobbing up and down, it was a child, waving for help.

Where had this child come from?

"HHHHeeeeeellllpp……." As the letters were emphasised he was trying to gasp for air. Never mind my fear of drowning. I jumped straight in without a second thought. Without even thinking about it, I don't know how but I somehow swam a few 100 yards which unfortunately was not close enough, I could feel the weight and tiredness of my legs slowing me down, trying to take me under the water.

I was going to fight it. I got close enough to grab his fingers then I couldn't hold myself above the water. I didn't even realise it that I was pulling him down under with me. I tried to shout;

"Hold on, grab my hand" as I shouted and tried to stay above the surface for air, hoping that Marc could hear me or at least realise I wasn't there.

I flapped my legs hoping I could float to the surface, the boy still hadn't gripped on to me. It was only a few minutes of struggling before I went under completely. My eyes were open wide, red with dread. Thoughts running through my head, I tried to scream, but bubbles were the only thing escaping my mouth.

What had I done? I took the boy down with me.

Everything went black! And Peaceful.

Still under the water, floating beneath the surface a shadow of a face began to appear in front of me. I felt tranquillity as each and every feature began to appear more and more prominent. With his long soft eyelashes, sparkly eyes and golden, brown, wavy hair. Plus a little cheeky grin on his face as he blew me a kiss, waved and then he just disappeared.

"AAAAHHHH!!!!....." I awoke from the sofa, screaming.

The husband ran down the stairs.

"Baby, baby are you okay" he stood over me with his still shadow, staring. He began to shake me.

"Wake up, wake up" he shouted in terror.

All of a sudden I gasped for air, my whole body flung forward, I struggled to breathe, I kept repeating the same thing, over and over again.

"He's gone! He's gone! He's gone! He's gone!" It all happened so quickly.

My husband just grabbed me and held me tight. I couldn't even hear the silent tears of my husband with my hysterical outburst. I could not control myself. I was soaked from head to toe. I looked down over his shoulder to see a pool of blood. I couldn't quite believe it, I placed my hand in to check if it was water, trying to make myself believe my mind was playing tricks on me.

I lifted my hands towards my face and reality had actually hit. It was blood. I could not be consoled.

"I'm taking you to the hospital, it might be nothing", as he wiped away his tears and wrapped a blanket round me and lifted me to the car.

We went in to see the doctor immediately, as he rubbed the gel on my stomach for the ultrasound, I felt a dark cloud pass over me. I just kept on muttering to myself "he's gone, he's gone".

Yet the doctor would not look up at me directly, he turned round to look at the nurse, shook his head once and then the nurse began to wipe my stomach to remove the excess gel. As she lifted my top back down to cover my stomach. The doctor said;

"I am sorry to say that unfortunately your baby is no longer with us, you have a still born baby, which means that...."

I never let him finish.

"I know what it means, he didn't make it".

I wanted to cry so much, but I couldn't completely register what was going on, it was all happening so fast.

The doctor said, "I am going to advise you see a Counsellor or attend a support group, there will be decisions you will need to make with regards to the birth, I can ask the nurse to go through the options with you, let me give you some time together'.

"She already has a Counsellor, she had one more session left until this happened" said the husband.

"Well I suggest you see our resident Counsellor, I think it will be a great deal of help moving forward, we can ask her to come and see you before you go for a brief chat, there are support groups you can also attend, with other families in a similar situation".

I couldn't focus or think of anything else right now. Was it my fault? Has all this travelling done something to my baby? The worse thought was that I had to go through the next few days to give a still birth. That is torture in itself, looking at my reflection, wishing he was still there. How am I going to cope?

"It was a boy wasn't it?".

He looked at me with a silent nod and then just held me.

As soon as we got home, I ran straight to the living room and began rummaging through the drawers. I found what

I was looking for, pencil and paper. I pulled it out and frantically started etching.

"Honey, what are you doing?" the husband shouted at me, yanking at my shoulder.

'"I'm trying to recreate his face, I saw him, I met our baby boy, I know it!, I know it was him!. I can't forget it. All I have is this memory, I have to get it on the paper".

I couldn't do it! I ended up screwing up the paper and throwing it across the room.

I think my husband was hoping the counselling sessions would cure me, I was dreading it. Dealing with my feelings wasn't the easiest thing for me to do, never mind sharing with someone else. At least with Lana we didn't talk a lot. (The husband didn't know that).

The Birth;

It wasn't even 24 hours later; the day I was induced for the stillbirth. I never slept, I couldn't.

We had to make so many decisions. I was not in the best frame of mind. I carefully packed my bag in the nursery, I struggled as I carefully folded in a custard yellow Babygro with matching booties along with a blanket and a monkey bear the husband had placed at the end of the already made cot.

I left the room without looking back and shut the door behind me. Walking down the stairs to the car felt like my last walk, to death row.

I was particular in what I wore, I chose to wear white to celebrate the life that would have been rather than mourn (it was not as easy as I thought).

Tears streamed and streamed down my drawn out, lifeless face but I kept my tears silent, trying not to show my pain as I was induced. Laying there on the bed, waiting for my baby to appear but not to be able to take him home was breaking me inside. There was sweat pouring down my face with tears of pain, and heartbreak as my husband squeezed my hand.

I knew that I had to see him there was no doubt about that, I couldn't live without seeing his handsome face. I tried to hold back on my grief as he was delivered and I couldn't hear his cry, I sat up waiting for the nurse to say they got it wrong, I closed my eyes for a moment, praying he would just cry. But he didn't! It was just too real.

The nurse took him to the other side of the room cleaned him and put on his clothes then wrapped him up in the cotton blanket my Nan had knitted. The silence in the room was intolerable.

The nurse brought him over to me, she looked at me awaiting a nod. I took him in my arms immediately and cradled his fragile body against my chest. This was the toughest thing I would ever endure. I rocked him back and forth in my arms.

"Meet your daddy Kris, you have his glistening eyes and his cute nose. Always remember as you watch down on us that we love you, each time I open my eyes and each time I close them you will be there, never will you be forgotten".

I didn't want to let go of him. My husband just stood over us and kissed him on his forehead. I kissed him all over his face, held his hand not wanting to let go. As I gave him back to the nurse, the husband turned away, I could tell he was trying to fight the tears like the strong man he's trying to be for me.

The nurse placed him in the cot and took him out. I cried uncontrollably, the husband lay on the bed next to me and held me.

The hospital had taken ink prints of his hands and feet, as we left the hospital I placed them with his scan in a box, I closed the lid and gripped onto the box.

I kept the box on the coffee table where I could see it all the time. I was withdrawn from reality, I spent most of my days on the couch staring at the box. Other days I would block everything out and I would stress, trying to remember what happened. I wanted the pain to stop.

Chapter 6
The Sessions

Going to regular bereavement counselling sessions was difficult. The Counsellor was empathetic, she encouraged me to express my emotions and feelings, yet for the first few weeks I was determined to sit there in silence. (I wasn't ready to attend group sessions) I couldn't bring myself to say how I felt, especially with this tiny hollow bump looking up at me. I could not comprehend what was happening.

I could not complain about her at all, the more she spoke the more I began to trust her. She then suggested that my husband attended with me (he denied at the beginning, he's too stubborn to say yes).

After a few weeks, I again tried to persuade him.

"Baby, please will you come with me, the counsellor said it will be good for us both to deal with our emotions together, if not for yourself for me, I need you", I looked at him with genuine tears.

"Okay, okay.....for you".

The first 4 weeks, I began writing a journal with how I felt as I struggled to express them. So the official session began with us both, I had decided I should be open with them both.

I was gripped to my diary, playing with the pages, slowly tearing pieces off, creating paper snow at my feet, while my husband's hand lay on my leg (showing me his support).

"So Misha, let's begin with you, do you want to start by sharing with us what you have written in your diary over the past few weeks. You don't have to read it all, you can read snippets", she said in her sympathetic tone.

Hesitantly I began.

"Well...." I paused.

"Well…. I think over time many issues have made me the way I am, I have to understand that I can't blame anyone apart from myself, how I turned out. I have struggled with alcohol abuse, depression, amongst other things you wouldn't understand…."

"Share it with us then baby, we may be able to understand and we can help one another through this" said the husband.

"I don't think we will ever get through this. The pain will always remain, it's about hiding the pain from the world and controlling it so it doesn't continuously resurface and affect our lives. I know I haven't dealt with my issues, which would normally be expected, but I'm trying. If I wasn't the way I am then the baby would still be alive, I don't mind to be punished for my failures and mistake's I have made, but why punish this innocent child", As I rubbed my stomach.

"I don't know if you would understand or even believe what I tell you, but please don't be angry, I am never in the right frame of mind, I sometimes feel so lonely, even in a room full of people, I feel so lost!".

"Be angry about what Misha?" Said the Counsellor.

"I, I……. Well I have been having an affair!".

The room went silent, I moved my eyes to the left to check my husband's reaction, but he didn't even flinch, I waited a moment, then I repeated it again.

"Did you not hear me, I have been having an affair!" as my tone and pitch raised a few more decibels'.

He then huffed and puffed away to himself, I didn't understand why he wouldn't say anything, then he perked up.

"Sorry, Dr……"

Before he continued I sharply interrupted him;

"Why are you sorry for? You don't need to be sorry for me, I can at least take that responsibility myself!", I said in a fury of rage.

"Sorry Dr, she has not been having an affair, I know she has not, I didn't think we would bring this up, seen as we have...... Misha has Dissociative Identity Disorder".

He then looked at me direct; "her identity is fragmented into two personalities, distinct to her only, she has been seeing a Holistic Counsellor, I have been trying to manage this with her, it has been a struggle, but I love her, I would do anything to support her".

I didn't want to hear any of his crap. I arose to my feet in a hot temper.

"Liar! Liar!...what the hell are you on about, there's nothing wrong with me, I'm telling you I'm having an affair, I can travel to other points in time, I know I can, why would I lie? Why would I lie?".

I then walked out and slammed the door behind me.

"It's all a figment of her imagination Dr, the affair whom she calls Marc that is me! I am not only her husband, but her affair! We are the same person. We do role play, it's the only way I can see this not to be an illness. She calls it 'travelling'. I honestly don't know where to start, she hears voices, and sometimes I catch her talking to herself. She is depressed, self-harms and an insomniac. I have to admit, it is taking its toll on me, but I love her. I am giving her pills to help with the insomnia and depression, I see her taking them, but I don't see any difference".

"Okay" said the doctor. "I think we should leave it there for today, I can put you in touch with someone to give you further support" as she scribbled down notes.

From here onwards at the remaining sessions, which I continued to attend, I agreed with everything they told me, just to get through it. Knowing in my mind they are against me, making up such ludicrous things.

My husband continued to give me pills, he watched me take them, but I always held them at the back of my throat until he turned his head. I then disposed of them down the sink or flushed them down the toilet.

I ticked all the boxes anything to end the sessions quicker. They thought I was getting better, but maybe I will always be like this.

I will never forgive myself for what has happened, I feel responsible. I won't lie, it scares the hell out of me to ever have to give birth again. Kris lives in my heart forever. I didn't think that I will ever be able to move on with my life.

Somehow I tried. Every day was different. The next few years we had ups and downs. I don't know how my husband stood by me for so long. I could never express how much he meant to me.

Although I believe my husband thinks I am still unwell, I tried my hardest to prove him wrong, so as the years had passed my travelling had slowed down.

My crazy, spontaneous days out with Marc were not so frequent, but when we did have them, I revelled in the moments. He just never wanted to settle down! I did eventually fall pregnant again with TWINS! Life was not so slow anymore and I thought my travelling stopped but had it really only just begun?

And I don't just mean school runs! I was always exhausted, but again struggled to sleep properly and I even thought about self-harming again but when I felt strongly to do so I always picked up Kris' prints and the urges stopped. In a way he saved me on a daily basis. He kept me focused on my future and the twins.

Frazzled 6 years later......dreaming again or not? Or have I relapsed?

Chapter 7
Reality Vs Dreams

I was drenched in the moment of this monsoon, it was beautiful. The beat of the drums as I was about to cross all the limits, embraced in this shower of love.

Then... Slam, went the door. I was awake.

I never wanted moments like this to end, who does?

The chimes of realisation, just like my alarm, late for work again!

Always dazing in and out of reality, as I place one foot in front of another, again for a tedious day behind the desk, we have to start somewhere.

Leaving the echo of each splash behind me as I ran for the bus, walking past the old man, to sit behind him. At least today he changed his shirt, however the stench of wet dog and odour of cigar still lingered.

The headphones safely plugged in, the silence was serene, as I nodded off.

Each drop was like a pearl as it slipped down my pure white silk shirt, stood under what felt like a waterfall. The smooth but slow trickle ran down my left cheek, like a puff of cold smoke was blown at me.

I then fell over…. Should I say pushed off my seat. "Excuse me, this is my stop".

My journey I must say, is usually this eventful. Before I knew it I was ushered to the window seat, the condensation streaming down my face.

Again I closed my eyes, tiredness seems to catch up with me, constantly falling asleep.

Each droplet was like a particle of sheer bliss, a unique moment as they tipped off the end of my pouting lips. There was no amount of electric that could pierce open my eyes to see what stood in front of me. I could only focus on the slow repetitive rhythms' of the drum in the background. Increasing in volume each moment, at the same time as my swaying hips, to and fro, with no cares in the world.

The bus had suddenly braked, my whole body flung forward.

The scent of…. Cigars and wet dog slowly disappeared. I forced my way through and between the many buggies' to step off the bus straight into a mini flood, or should I say puddle! Only to realise I ran out the house in my torn, rugged slippers. "What the hell! I'm comfy!" Good job I keep my heels under my desk.

I forgot to mention, my journey had only begun, and this was a daily occurrence. I still have a train to catch. The kids were taken care of by my husband.

Running up each step, hopping between everyone else rushing to their station, ensuring not to have my slippers torn away from my bare, unpainted dry feet.

Just typical! Reaching into my pocket, it was empty! I looked down and realised I'm still wearing my fluffy; polka dot nightgown, "what the hell!".

I had an inside pocket! Scrunched between my hair bobble and used handkerchief, there it was my money. Only to be greeted head first into a queue and the slap around the face of potpourri. Yes, the good old favourite of some, lavender and pungency of rosemary, lingering which once I loved rubbed into a nice rump of lamb... the Rosemary that is.

(Make sure you keep with all this drifting between two worlds).

There it was the aroma that attracts lovers, even worlds apart. Just as insects are attracted to the sweet nectar, I too was intrigued. Along with my swaying hips and the constant beats of the drum, getting ever so much closer, I started to lift my size 6 feet to tap away. The coarse grains of sand, which sifted between my toes.

I daren't open my eyes, to a restless intoxicated world, which is what usually lay under my always heavy eyelids; a black cloud.

As the drum phased out, I was focused on my throbbing yet poetic heart, a soul in itself.

As I lifted my steady, slightly olive tanned hands, the sand slipped through my moisturised fingers and fell so soft back down, a pin could have been dropped and I was none the wiser. You can understand why I was so hesitant in opening my eyes, the fear which always lived beyond the surface, like a prickly thorn, on once my favourite flower.

Now I wasn't scared! I began to slowly peel open my gentle eyes, where droplets of pure blue sea seeped through and ran down the side of my nose. There I was stood in paradise, where else would I be?

"Next... Yes, we are waiting, there is a queue behind you, speak now or move along" said the frantic lady behind the ticket desk.

I'm the one stood waiting, and now of course, I am causing all the havoc.

"Yes a return please", I said in a patronizing tone.

"Where too?".

She said, in her husky voice. I Paused. Why doesn't she know where I am going, she ought to by now. She issues me a ticket at least three times a week, which is usually how many times I leave my monthly ticket on the ledge in the front room.

I grabbed my ticket, and made my way down the never ending escalators. As I approached the bottom, I bent down to reach for my ticket I just dropped, before it was consumed by the moving metal beneath my feet.

Oh yes...here, stumbling off the bottom step of the escalators where the thread I had been meaning to tear from the back of my slipper, almost got ravelled in the mechanism.

As you can probably already tell, I am in and out of reality and the dream world, my imagination is beyond description. I hope you can keep up!

Chapter 8
Cake

Looking up at the screen, platform 11... fantastic, I have time to sip on a skinny soya mocha, and people watch. Watching the world pass me by on fast-forward, which is sometimes how my life feels. Wouldn't you just love to rewind as if the present never happened, even re-write it?

Sipping on my mocha, piping hot! I must have nodded off again.

Just as the sun is glaring on my back, I peer down with my blue ocean eyes to see I am wearing my favourite nightdress, you know? The one you wear when you are "in the mood', to make yourself feel 'one in a million".

Yes, Royal blue chiffon with a deep V neck which just stopped short of my upper rib and covered most, sorry some of my voluptuous breasts. It was tight fitted across my chest and flowed down to my bony ankles.

The vibration of violin strings echoed, synchronising with my heart, I walked a few steps over the silky, warm sand back into the initially cool but gradually warm, comforting water. Jumping, splashing, my wavy luscious red locks swaying, I aim for the waterfall.

It was like a thousand destinations and journeys', like a song that was forever on repeat, along with the flame at the pit of your stomach, not one to be wary about, but to await the smoke to arise from some part of my body, seeping darkness with it. With a sigh of relief, any worries flew away.

Splashing with circular movements with my whole body, throwing the ripples of wavy, ice colour, blue water over my face, I suddenly lost my balance. In slow motion I fell back into a familiar pair of hands, which always gripped my body in such a way I got butterflies in the pit of my stomach.

I tilted my head back ever so slightly as I opened my eyes, (which had automatically shut when I lost my balance), to see my husband. He was always there when I needed him. I knew it was a dream, I never got to kiss him goodbye this morning due to my hurried exit.

I regained my posture to turn around and peck him on the cheek, as I swung around with my 8 stone body, he was gone! Just typical, as you get to the best part in your dream, it's over! Well not in this dream.

I decided to venture around in my paradise...

"Sorry to interrupt you, may I sit? All the tables are taken, I can't bear to stand any longer in these heels, at least until my train is due".

"Not a problem", I said.

As she lay her ticket on the table top with one hand, she used her other hand to remove her wispy, I must say slightly dry hair from her face and tucked it behind her ears. She sat down with the sound of her feet slipping out of her fake leather shoes with a deep sigh of momentarily relief. I did however notice we were taking the same train from her ticket. She did look familiar, in a way she reminded me of my sister, but I didn't think to ask her name.

I took a rather large gulp of my mocha, glaring at the screen, six minutes until the train departs. I do not want to be stared at this morning in my apparently unnoticeable poke a dot gown. I need a seat for my 33 minute journey, but of course a few more minutes in paradise would be amazing.

Such a high step on to the train, the gap between the train and platform as usual was wide enough for a half me to fall through. Tightly scrunching my toes at the top of my slippers, ensuring I don't lose them to the tracks, I stepped onto the train. 'Great a window seat'.

Just as the train departed, the trolley man as I called him appeared;

"Tea?" He cleared his throat; then again, "do you want tea?" As I took a double take with my eyes, still half a sleep.

"Oh yes, please, do you have cake?" I said.

"Does it look like I have cake?"

"Well if I knew I wouldn't have asked, would I? Just the tea then… please".

To be honest I don't know why I asked, knowing full well that it's not at an all you can eat buffet, it's just a trolley!

Back to my dream world….

I stumbled onto the grainy, peach coloured gravel behind me to see floral tables and chairs set up like a tea party. Yet there were no people. I walked over to one of the tables where there was a hot steamy pot of tea, I lifted the lid, shut my eyes and inhaled. Oooh my favourite Earl Grey, so I pulled out the chair and sat down.

I poured myself a cup full and puffed away into my China teacup to try and cool down this piping hot Earl Grey tea, and yes my right pinky is curled and pointed out, what else would you expect? I then placed it back on the slightly imperfect saucer. To my astonishment, cake!

Not just any cake but lemon drizzle cake, it was so soft it just melted in my mouth, I savoured each bite like it was my last. Now this is what I am talking about, who needs public transport?

Cake always made a bad day at work seem a whole lot brighter, it used to be biscuits, but you know how difficult it is just to consume only one biscuit at one time, this is where the pounds piled straight on to my hips! But hey this is my dream; I also reached for a couple of biscuits.

I dipped my biscuit in my tea, as usual a piece fell straight in and sank to the bottom of the cup.

"Here use this". I looked up and my gran passed me a silver teaspoon. She always knew what to do, to be honest who doesn't like a soggy (digestive) biscuit. She rubbed her hand over my hair and sat down to join me. As she did the gravelled area began to fill with people, an atmosphere of pure enjoyment, laughter, giggles, ladies dancing, men playing poker.

It was lovely to share such a loving moment with such a special woman. Laughing and giggling so hard that the lines on my face felt like they were burning.

There were tones of rhythmical joy in the background, as I turned my slightly wet, almost dry head to soak in the atmosphere, it was like I was sat in an open café, with people from all walks of life. It was like an afternoon tea party of pure pleasure and distraction. Being here was so unpredictable, whatever was going to happen next?

"Next Station!"

Echoed in my right ear. I opened my eyes to look out the window, "fog"; I looked up at the every so slow ticking clock, 11 minutes to my station. Back to it.

The infectious sound of roaring laughter filled the air with happiness. It was contagious, it united all the people that surrounded me; family and friends, no one was a stranger. As Herman Melville once said;

'I know not all that may be coming, but be it what it will, I'll go to it laughing'.

Taking the last bite of my; first covered blackberry jam then topped with cream scone, I licked my Scarlett red lips and continued to sip my tea until it was gone.

What always came with laughter was children;
'It's the children the world almost breaks who grow up to save it' (Frank Warren).

How inspirational, but true.

I could faintly hear them, but they were not in sight. Maybe it was that baby three seats down, weeping on the train.

I have two young children, the sweetest children you could imagine (I guess as parents we are biased). Like fairies that you don't want to grow up (and leave home) they spread magic in a simple smile.

Millie and Maya, twins. I must say intelligent 6 year olds. They love to read, sing and dance, which child doesn't. With toasty brown, naturally wavy hair and a fair complexion. Dusky brown eyes and eyelashes that would make any parent swoon. The only way you could tell them apart was that Millie had a birth mark on the back of her neck.

They were not just twins, sisters but best friends, they had such a strong bond that when one of them shed a tear, the other wiped them away and a warm hug gave you that tingly heart felt moment that you felt protected from the outside world.

Maybe that was the sound of their laughter and giggles I heard earlier.

I poured myself another cup of tea. Gossiping away with my gran was my favourite pastime; we were never short of conversation. Days could pass and we would never know.

Gran then pulled out her knitting; she loved to knit especially for the girls. Millie loves pastille pink and Maya, Lilac. She was knitting them an elegant patch blanket with these colours. The girls never slept apart from one another and I doubt they would sleep without this blanket, especially the quaint ribbon that was woven across each side of it.

How I wanted to embrace both my girls in my arms in this moment.

To be honest I was quite partial to some knitting, I was making them both a shawl each in their favourite colours. Amongst other knitwear, socks, cardigans, yes I was always a bit over the top. I wasn't quite at the stage of adding buttons and ribbons, but I am sure I will get there eventually. It's the thought that counts.

Chapter 9
The Journey Continues

As the tannoy loudly awoke me; "Last station" echoed.

I shot up, straight out of my seat. I don't usually fall asleep during my journey, maybe the kids kept me awake last night.

Such a cold chill as I stepped onto the platform, with my left foot first.

"Sorry" as the 30 something, (I must say) good looking male stood on the back of my right slipper, almost tumbling over trying to regain my posture.

Why is everyone in such a rush? You would think the world was about to end. And I thought I was the only one living in my own world! Making a fast pace down the stoney platform towards the exit sign, I'm just glad I have underwear on beneath this fluffy nightgown.

I finally made it out of the station; luckily my office was only a 5-minute walk away. Straight into a puddle, yet again, this is becoming a bad habit. You think I would have learnt my lesson by now. I have no choice really, it was pouring down, I ran like there was no tomorrow.

Rain can be quite relaxing especially when sat in a conservatory on your own, eyes closed, and a clear mind. The sounds of pattering feet, fluttering down the roof. Honestly it is soothing! On the other hand a romantic dinner for two, along with a soft light, your favourite tune in the background and that tingly feeling down your spine, just as if it is a first date. A tight embrace with my husband, an embrace I never wanted to leave.

I felt safe.

I made it with five minutes to spare, I jumped into the revolving doors, as usual I spun round twice before stumbling out, straightening myself before anyone saw. I swept past Bob and Henry, our security guards; I don't know what they usually do, apart from drink coffee and eat donuts. They even let me through, dressed like this. Bob even gave me that uncomfortable right wink as he does every morning.

I squeezed myself through the sliding doors of the lift, with the same old people, stinky Dave from Accounts on 3rd and miss 'I ate all the biscuits' on 9th, even with crumbs down her blouse from what looked like she shovelled in prior to getting in the lift, as her jaw looked like it was on overtime.

Standing in any lift always gave me the giggles, doesn't it make you want to burst into laughter? With these people who blame me! I have learnt to count to 10 without looking direct at anyone, trust me it's an art, just to stop myself bursting into a fit of laughter.

I made it out the lift, flicked the kettle on the way to my desk. Dropped my bottom on the soft cushioned seat, with a hard back, threw off my slippers under my desk and slipped my toes first into my black leather 3inch heals. "That's better". You could recognise my desk from space, it was like no other, a thick layer of dust where underneath (yes there is an underneath, somewhere!) imprints of tea stains. It used to be impeccably clean, once! However the picture of my family got me through a day here.

There was a variety of different people whom worked in my office, you had the whisperers, who gossiped amongst themselves as someone once said to me, *"it's not gossip if it's true"* It was all gossip! Whilst sometimes vindictive. Thinking that anyone out of their 'circle' couldn't hear them, but I could, my hearing was impeccable.

There were the 'goody two shoes'; the swots as they were known at school. Heads down, no time to even use the bathroom, in case they missed something vital! I mean what is there to miss in this office?

I wasn't grouped with anyone at the office, it was 'just me' I liked it that way.

Now you must be wondering what I do all day, apart from eat and drink (yes I admit it, I live for food).

'Cold calling', not the most glamorous, fun job you thought I might do, but it paid the bills (topped up nicely with my commission, I always exceeded my targets). It fed and clothed my kids and even paid for some luxury holidays. What more could I ask for?

Courtesy of Image Fusion

Chapter 10
Time to Explore

A few more cups of tea (and many biscuits too), it seemed hours had passed (there was no clock). Chatting with so many different people was interesting, it felt as if I knew them, our stories were similar in some sort of way. Nowadays most people don't have time to say hi never mind a chat, it was refreshing. I seemed to get on well with everyone here, there was no judgement or agenda.

Time to explore!

Over the other side of this beautiful open style café, there were many tropical evergreen palm trees from the banana tree, bearing so much fruit, to the eye catching traveller's palm, with the most unique leaf pattern you would have ever seen.

Animals roamed free with not a care in the world. Endangered animals that you have merely heard of. From the Golden-Bellied Capuchin to a Sumatran Tiger and the Yellow-Crested Cockatoo, which continuously pecked away at the banana tree. I must say the glass frog is stunning; there are no words to describe it but wow! (I knew the animal kingdom quite well).

I just perched on the end of a hand carved, rustic bench, watching nature pass by, a moment of pure bliss. Although secretly missing my two babies, in the background. (Yes, a bit of peace, makes me nervous).

The Sumatran Tigers were grazing directly in front of me, I was not scared at all. As they slowly plodded off in the opposite directions, I noticed an elegant gold veined, spiralled, marble staircase, which curved around nothingness. I was intrigued...

Beauty is an imperfection, that's what makes it so unique.

As I got closer I noticed the marble was sharply chipped in some places, this did not taint the beauty. As I placed my right foot first, I awaited the burst of coldness to hit the sole of my foot, and there was a pair of open toe sandals wrapped around my once bare feet. With white crisscross straps and a tiny blue flower on the buckle.

I had mixed emotions about what lay ahead, a deep sigh of excitement before I continued with my second step.

Still walking up these spiral stairs, I wondered what lay at the top. I began to feel a shudder of coldness trickle down my spine, the hairs on my neck stood up on end (that's because there was no hair below my neck) I think it was the excitement.

Luckily I was now wearing a satin nightgown, over my chiffon nightdress. It had the most gorgeous flowery, hand woven lace which ran down the arms and across the bustline, with floaty cuffs and hung just below my knees.

I felt like a princess, I was just missing my crown and Prince Charming. I do feel like I'm living in a fairy tale. The colours of my prayers are being slowly brought upon me, I knew I was close to seeing my family. No rules of this world could stop the gaze I wished to have with my husband.

I made it to the top!

I must say my dreams have never felt this real before. I stood on the greenest softest, grass you can imagine, it was so fresh and crisp. I was now back in a comfy pair of clean, untorn slippers.

What lay beyond the grass was magnificent, it was a bright field of yellow flowers, lilies, roses and tulips with a familiar smell of opal which swept pass me like a breath of air, the sound of a flickering candle burning in the distance made me feel like I was home, a sense of calmness came over me. I was curious to see where this smell would lead me, where was it coming from?

So I walked through this golden field of sunshine. Following the smell with the tip of my nose.

Brushing my satin gown between each flower felt quite sensual, like soft fingers running up and down my body. I picked up one of the lilies and placed it behind my left ear and picked a bunch of flowers, which I gripped in my right hand. I could then hear giggling again as if it was running away from me, I followed these sounds to the other side of the field.

I thought before I begin on my next path, I would enjoy this scenery. I lay on my back against of this quaint field, looking up at the blue sky, I watched the birds flutter over me.

Deep in thought I could then hear 'mum' being echoed from behind me, and rustling through the fields. I sat up and low and behold my two gorgeous babies ran out from nowhere.

"Mum, mum you made it", they said in uniformity.

"Where have you been, we've been waiting for you for ages", said Millie.

I just grabbed them both, with each arm and embraced them and lay as many kisses on their cheeks as I could.

"I was here babies, I have been looking for you".

Before I knew it they were running down the path, which lay in front of me, it was a wavy stone path, which led to a hill, above which there was a smokey effect waving through the sky.

"Millie...Maya, where are you going? Come back here!".

Within a blink of an eye they were gone. These kids really keep me on my toes. As I arose to my feet and made my way down the path. I felt as if someone placed their hand on my right shoulder, I turned around, there was no one there. It was time to begin my journey home. I must have been skipping down this path for about half an hour, chirping away to myself. I made my way up and back over the other side of the hill.

I came across a beautiful atmospheric park, it was built like a castle, an oasis for children. With trunks tables and log seats, a checkerboard picnic table where the adults were sat.

There was a net rope net bridge from one end of the castle to the other, with children swaying from one side to the other, with a floor water fountain underneath. The sound of joyous children made me smile, inside out.

I sat on the log seat, watching the children playing, when they fell they just got straight back up without any streams of tears, unlike my girls.

It was so relaxing watching them have fun, chasing each other with toy swords, up and down the slide, until a ball came flying towards me.

Ouch! As it hit me in the face, I began to rub my forehead, as I pulled away my hand, there was the cutest boy stood in front of me glaring at me with his slightly tilted head, with a sorry look on his face. He had blue eyes with small pigments of green, with long fluttering eyelashes. His golden brown hair limped over his right cheek. He was wearing denim dungarees with red sneakers.

"It's okay sweetie, it was an accident, come here let me tie up your shoe lace".

I picked him up and sat him on my left knee and just as I finished tying the bow, he grabbed me tight around my neck just like my girls do and then gave me a big kiss on my left cheek before jumping off to return to playing with his ball.

I had the strangest feeling at the bottom of my stomach, maybe it's my motherly nature. It was the moment he looked in my eyes, he just stole my heart. For some reason I felt that I had met him before, but it's not possible. I sat for a while laughing and giggling watching the children play before continuing down the path.

It started to get nippy and I began to shiver. The weather had suddenly changed, it was snowing. As I wrapped my arms around my upper body to keep myself warm, I was now wearing a pure white long velvet coat, with the whitest of white fur cuffs. The wedged knee length boots, covered my bare skin.

'Boy, does this weather change'.

The feeling of the snow as it fell on my face was indescribable, I closed my eyes and opened my mouth, as I looked up and twirled on the spot I pulled out my tongue and allowed the snow to melt gently into nothingness. The snow always gave me a sense of calmness, all my worries just disappeared.

It was odd the way the weather and surroundings were changing around me, I just enjoyed every moment as if it was my last.

Courtesy of Image Fusion

Chapter 11
The Cottage

Low and behold, it was a cottage, my cottage! Just as I had always wanted.

Blue bricks (yes, not your everyday typical red brick) lay the path to the picket pink fence.

As I opened the fence to the left was a well preserved herb garden, with chives, coriander, lemon thyme and my favourite rosemary, amongst many more.

To the right of the fence was a vegetable patch, courgettes, cauliflower, carrots and potatoes.

The front of the cottage was covered in vibrant flowers, woven around the cottage like an art display, you couldn't even see the bricks that it was built with, that's the way I liked it. It was very inviting, with a homely feel.

I took a step to the banana colour door (I know, don't judge, If you saw it you would surely fall in love with it, honest!) which was slightly opened.

"Hello, hello is anyone here?" There was no response.

There was that welcoming smell of opal in the air. I stepped in on to the natural polished wood floor, a cool breeze swooshed passed me.

It was peaceful and calm. I walked into the living room to the left of the front door, to see Maya and Millie's smiles hung on the centre of the wall above the burning wood fire place. The quaint cream wool rug covered the centre of the room with a tree top, style coffee table placed on the top.

I looked into the full-length mirror, which I had always wanted, in my living room. I closed my eyes and twirled on the spot, as I opened them, I was now wearing a delicate, sweetheart, strapless flowery dress with a cerise ribbon which cinched in my waist. With a pair of 3 inch lilac stilettos, (I rarely had time to wear heels) these were actually very comfortable, I could quite happily clean the house in these. The curls in my hair were such defined ringlets which were pinned up at the back of my head, where a few curls fell in front of my face so naturally. I really felt like a princess now.

Of course the girls toys were everywhere, which I tipped toed over like hot coals, trying not to trip as usual. I then heard the floorboards creak above me.

"Hello, husband, are you up there?" Even after all these years this is how I still referred to him.

There was no response. As soon as I stood on the first step, *SLAM* went the back door. I went to investigate......

There was no one there.

I get distracted so easily. I walked into the kitchen. To me the kitchen is the heart of any home; this is where magic is created. I would be my most happiest when I was baking, and even better when I saw that everyone really enjoyed my food.

Wooden floors throughout the cottage gave the place a warm welcome feeling, the kitchen tops were rustic yet vintage. Even the kitchenware was eclectic, with that shabby chic effect. It was quirky. The toaster was green, an old fashioned whistling kettle was fashionable yet unique. There wasn't a traditional oven but an open fire built with brick, fantastic for homemade pizza in particular (the kids favourite). There was no need for a microwave, no ping meals here!

I could hear the floor boards creak above me again. This time I decided I would venture all the way to the top.

I opened the first door to the right of the stairs, it was a reader's heaven, a library filled with books from the floor to the ceiling. There was a chocolate brown worn 3 piece sofa which lay in front of the full length window which looked out to the side of the cottage. Where there was a magnificent waterfall, just like the one I was stood in at the beginning of my journey. It seemed peaceful, yet soothing, a haven for those who want to escape. With the odd humming bird outside.

Intrigued to the noises I keep hearing I slowly opened the door to the second room.

There he was in the kingsize bed, with a pure white silk duvet. His right hand over the side of the bed, one leg under the duvet and the other over the top, clutching to the duvet as if I was going to steal it. Yes that is usually what I did each time I turned back and forth in bed, somehow I would take the duvet with me leaving him bare skinned and icy cold. It's not my fault I can't get comfortable is it!

I didn't want to disturb him, he looked ever so comfortable. I just stood there for a few moments and watched him. As my heart fluttered as if it was our first date (this is how I felt each time I saw him).

Quietly without waking him I walked round to the empty side of the bed, my side of the bed! I reached with my right hand over my shoulder to unzip my dress from behind, I wiggled out of my dress with much ease and then slipped my feet out of my shoes.

I was stood bear with a simple pair of tie sided thongs, made with elegant black satin and ivory ribbon ties. Easy to pull off, even for a man! I obviously had no bra on with the strapless dress, my perky breasts didn't need help to stay up (no issues unhooking either).

I lifted the top corner of the duvet, and slowly crept into the bed, with my lukewarm body. I edged closer to him, my nipples dug into his back at the same time as I threw my right arm around his tight chest. I held tight on to his toned body. This was my safe place. I linked my fingers between his and he gripped tightly, digging my overgrown nails into his left palm.

Before I knew it his right arm was back under the duvet, running down the top of my thigh down my leg, as far as his arm could reach, back up in-between my legs, teasing his fingers over my satin underwear. He slowly tugged on the ivory ribbon, I awaited him to pull it open.

He used the ribbon to pull his weight partly over my body, his chest sunk into mine. Softly, softly kissing my skin from my neck, down to my stomach, he gradually tugged on the ivory ribbon which he was gripped onto with his left hand, then slid his hand over to the other side and untied the second ribbon. He opened his eyes and looked straight into mine. If looks could kill, his always kept me alive!

There was a magic spell on my heart, it was pounding, we were about to lose our consciousness. His dark eyes always entangled me with black magic that lay beyond the surface.

After our passionate reunion, I was in the comfort of my loved one, feeling safe was the best feeling ever. I turned over to my side and just watched my husband sleep as happy tears ran down my face. And hearing the girls playing outside. I felt so blessed.

I had once again fallen asleep (this was getting to be a habit) oddly this time I didn't fall into my dreams, I felt like I was finally living it.

I was awoken by pattering footsteps, like a herd of animals up the stairs, then the door flung open.

"Mum, mum we missed you" said my beautiful girls.

They jumped straight into the bed, crawled under the duvet and grabbed me tight. One around my neck, the other attached to my arm.

"We've been waiting for you, we want to eat your food" said Millie.

"Dad can't cook" said Maya.

Don't I know it, I thought to myself, I bet he made pasta.

"All he has made us is pasta" said Maya.

I giggled to myself.

"Look at your hair girls, you are full of mud, and these beautiful dresses are torn" as I ran my fingers through Millie's hair, pulling out twigs. They looked like they had been to war.

Can you believe my husband was still asleep, he always slept through the girls crying since they were born.

"Come and play with us mum" said Millie with a smile ear to ear.

They jumped straight off the bed and downstairs out the back door as it slammed behind them. I really don't know where they get their energy from, must be all that pasta!

With a moment to think, it just clicked to me that the girls said they missed my food! I hadn't been anywhere had I? I was beginning to doubt myself. (It's only a dream!).

"Honey, honey, wake up!" As much as I loved to watch him sleep, I loved it even more waking him up.

"Let's go play with the kids" I said to him.

"Hmmmmm" as he turned over with his back to me.

"Come on" as I shook his body, like one of the kids. I helped push him gently out of bed, his legs flopped out the side of the bed first, followed by his body. He sat on the edge of the bed, yawned and stretched with his arms over his head, he leaned his head back to peck me on the cheek.

I slipped out of my side of the bed and stepped back into my dress, zipped myself up and attempted to make myself look half decent.

As I walked round to the end of the bed my husband just grabbed me, kissed my right cheek, placed the straggly piece of hair behind my ear and whispered "come back to bed, I have missed all of this". As he pulled me towards his bare body.

"What do you mean?" as I took a step back and pulled myself away from him.

"Well, tell me? You and the girls seem to talk in riddles".

I waited for a response. "TELL ME!!" I shouted again.

Chapter 12
Something is not right

5pm, work finished, finally! Time to go and start my 2nd job. My husband, the kids, my life! Cooking, cleaning and preparing for the next day, does it ever end?

I pulled out my phone to check my messages, usually from my husband. Oddly this was the first time I hadn't received one (usually to tell me he loves me). I tried calling him but it went to voicemail! I didn't want to overthink it and worry as I would panic. I just thought it was odd. Leaving voicemail is impersonal, especially for a character like me.

So I texted.

Hope you picked up the girls from school okay.
On my way home.
Hope you had a great day, can't wait to see you.
Love You X

The journey home was pretty mundane, it always goes so much quicker for me than the journey to work (maybe that's because I am always dreaming on the way to work).

I unlocked the front door with keys that were in my left pocket. To be honest, I thought I ran out of the house without any keys this morning! Even I'm surprised.

All the curtains were drawn. I don't remember drawing them this morning. There didn't seem to be anyone home, ahhh....I just remembered it's Monday, kids are at swimming lessons tonight. I always had a fear of water since being a child, I have never gotten over my fear. I didn't want the kids to go through life with the same phobia.

I opened all the curtains in the living room, sank straight into the sofa (a quick half an hour to myself before the chaos begins) and clicked the red button on the remote, finally choosing a channel after surfing (okay flicking) channels, it was a bad habit!, Well deserved!

Again I nodded off. It must have felt like minutes and I woke up with a shiver, I wiped my eyes, looked up to see the curtains were drawn. That's odd! I am sure I shut them when I came in. I peered through the heavy velvet curtains and it was dark. Maybe I slept a while. I looked up at the large face clock staring back at me, the hands were stuck on 3 o'clock.

Something didn't feel right, when people say 'they can feel it in their bones' I began to experience this sensation.

I shook it off, time to prepare dinner I think, the kids will be starving by the time they get back from swimming! I walked into the kitchen, there was a cool breeze which made me shudder.

"Oh my God, where the hell is all the food?", as I frantically pulled open all the cupboards one by one. Even standing on my toes to look at the back of each bare cupboard.

The fridge was completely bare, so bare there wasn't even the half bottle of ketchup in the fridge door.

"What the hell is going on" I asked myself, "I feel like I'm going mad".

I grabbed my phone so quick, I don't even know how I unlocked the phone, my hands were shaking so much, I just lost total grip of it, and it fell. My reflexes were fast, I bent down and just caught it. There was no signal!

There was a panic which consumed my body, I couldn't control my breathing, it became heavier and deeper with each breathe I tried to grasp.

I ran back down the corridor and up the stairs, gripping to the staircase, trying not to lose balance in the panic. I flung open the twins room, in the back of my mind I could hear them say 'mum, we love you, we love you'. But the room was empty. The expectation of their smiles from the sight of my babies, turned into fear.

I paused for a moment. "Think, think!", I kept repeating to myself in my head.

I don't understand what's going on.

SLAM, went a door.

I turned around, everything seemed calm. I peered down the stairs and the front door was still shut. I edged towards the bannister, knelt down and sobbed. So many thoughts running through my mind.

"AAAAHHHH!!!!" I just screamed, I needed to let it all out, whatever it was!

I just wanted to see my family. Tears streamed down my face, as fast as I was wiping them away with the straggly ends of my nightgown. After a good weep, I got up and checked my bedroom. Empty!

I ran back down the stairs, almost tripping head first. I just regained my balance as I made it to the bottom step. A slouch on the sofa and consider my next few steps might help me figure out what to do next. The sofa was gone, there were no curtains, and the clock was the only item that remained. Can you believe it was now ticking?

SLAM. This time as I turned my head round to the left, I saw the front door open and slam shut.

"Whose there?!!" I shouted. No one responded.

I went to grab the handle of the front door, but it was jammed, my hand just kept slipping off the door knob.

I couldn't comprehend what was happening. The tears were now flowing like a river down my face. 'Breathe, breathe' I said to myself.

I sat on the stairs leaning against the barrister, gripped to it as if I was in a jail cell, with nowhere to escape, no air, and only my own shadow.

Again I tried the mobile phone, everyone I tried to call went direct to voicemail.

'Shadows go in front of you! Leading into your future and trail behind you! Leaving a part of you in the past. They are clearest when we are in the light and disappear when we lose ourselves in the darkness'

-Kiersten White.

I was lost! I just felt the world was passing me by and I had no control to pause or stop it for a while. I felt like a train ready to derail and there was no conductor to guide me.

I thought a nice bath might calm me down. I went back up to run myself a bath. As I went towards the closed door I could see steam whispering out from under the door. I opened the door....slightly hesitant. As I slowly pushed it inwards the door flung open, the bath was already running and there was no one there. I peered back out in the corridor, all that passed me was a wispy breeze.

The bath was filled with fluffy, lavender bubbles and there was a large glass of vino on the back of the bath tub. Just how my husband always prepared me a relaxing bath.

I sat on the edge of the bath and dropped my head into my hands and just sighed. After a few moments the taps had stopped running, I turned around, dropped my night gown on the floor, slipped into the bath and reached for the vino. I held the glass above the water as I submerged my head under, nothing felt any clearer under here, however it was an escapism. It was beginning to feel familiar.

I cried so much sipping away on wine, I had no more tears to wipe away. Slowly, slowly as I calmed down, I just nodded off. (This started to feel familiar) I dropped my glass on the floor, I heard the shatter resonate in the distance. But this time, my husband was not there to pick up the glass, and I went straight into a dream;

I was in the moment of this monsoon, it was beautiful, the beat of the drum as I was about to cross all the limits, embraced in this shower of love.

This is where it all began! Or is it?!

Chapter 13
The Truth

"Okay, okay, I will calm down, let me get some clothes on first then we can talk properly, over a cup of tea" said the husband.

As if a cup of tea solves everything! Sounds like I may need something stronger.

We both went down to the kitchen, as I passed the living room to the left, the sound of the clock resonated, the ticking seemed to get louder and louder and my surroundings were peaceful. Until the husband brushed past me into the kitchen, lifting his right arm into his jumper.

As I followed him into the kitchen, he pulled out the brandy bottle and gave it to me neat in a glass. Not even any ice!

I could hear the girls laughing and giggling, it sounded like they were running around, having fun. I put down my glass and opened the back door.

The garden was beautiful, it had everything you would dream of having, there was a stoney path which led the way to a large green double swing where there was what looked like a pond, but no fish!

Opposite the swing was a fountain, flowing with crystal blue water. The swing was made with worn out tyres and hung with rope, just like it was when I was a child.
The girls were climbing the spider web, red frame, "be careful girls" I shouted."

"We will mum".

You could tell this garden was loved and looked after, the flowers were blooming. I picked up a bunch of red roses between my right fingers and raised them to my face to smell. As I closed my eyes to inhale the scents of beauty, the husbands touch to my left shoulder made me pause. He grabbed my hand and we sat on the picnic bench behind the fountain.

My husband began to clear his throat as he handed me my brandy.

"Where shall I start" he said trembling.

"The beginning might be a good place" as I squeezed his hand. He swirled his glass of brandy before taking a large swig.

It was a Sunday morning, the twin's birthday. As usual the birthday girls decide what they want to do. Boy did they have a big day planned.

6am, both girls ran into our room and jumped on the bed, jumping up and down, pulling the duvet off us.

"Can we have our presents now, please, please, please?".

The husband continued….

….You were out like a light, you didn't sleep well at all, and you were tossing and turning most of the night.

"Come on girls, go and put some clothes on, then we will go downstairs and open your presents, that's if you can find them, we will let your mum sleep a bit longer".

I pecked you on the cheek and tucked you back in and quietly shut the door behind me smiling as I saw you sleeping so peacefully. You are always so beautiful as you sleep.

The girls were so excited and you were fast asleep, I couldn't let them wait any longer to open their presents.

They found their presents so quick, they tore the wrapping to shreds all over the floor. I made them blueberry pancakes for breakfast whilst they were shovelling it in, I slowly crept upstairs with a tray for you with a glass of freshly squeezed orange juice and some pancakes.

"Yes, they were lovely I remember eating them, they were so fluffy, with the extra sweetness of honey, I could eat some now" said Misha.

Yes once I managed to tear you away from your sleep. After eating I gave you a couple of painkillers for your migraine. You are such a fighter, you managed to get yourself out of bed, and usually you struggled when you had a migraine.

"Yes, I didn't want to let my babies down" Misha replied.

I ran you a steamy bath, filled with lots of bubbles, just the way you like it, with a few scented candles. After letting the kids play out in the garden I came up. "With a mug of earl grey, my favourite", as Misha interrupted.

(We always finish each other's sentences).

You sipped on your tea whilst having a soak, in the meantime I got the girls ready.

"Come on baby, we need to go and pick up your mum" I shouted up the stairs. You dragged your body down the stairs, with your right hand lagging behind you on the bannister. You came to the bottom step, pulled down your sunglasses to the end of your nose and said with that sorry look on your face.

"Can you not go and pick me up in a few hours, I don't feel a 100%".

"Please Honey, just try and hang in there for a couple of hours, for the girl's sake, they are too excited.

I grabbed you with my right arm and lifted you off the step, and kissed them soft cheeks of yours. You always melt my heart, even more so when you don't feel well.

"Right, girls, let's start this day off, let's go and pick up Nana, then I'm going to thrash you all at bowling, burgers and lots of cake!".

"Yeahhhh", shouted the girls.

We got in the car. The girls were playing with their toys in the back, screaming and kicking the back of your seat as usual. But this time you didn't shout at them. I could tell you were not well.

We got to your mums, as soon as she opened the door you ran straight passed her, almost knocking her over. You ran straight up the stairs and we heard the door slam.

"Stay here girls, let me get your mum and Nan".

I ran upstairs after you and banged on the door "Baby, are you okay?" All I could here was you vomiting, "Baby……".

"Yes, I am fine Honey, I will be a few minutes, please just give me a few minutes" said Misha.

To be honest you have been feeling down and sick for weeks now, I just thought it was your migraines, you really suffered more than most. I stood outside the bathroom waiting for you with a glass of water and the kids were in the car.

Your mum came up, "Is she okay", she whispered.

"I can hear you, behind this door, and yes I am fine, please give me 5 minutes and I will be down, go and start the car" you said in a trembling voice.

After a few minutes you came out to the car still with your sunglasses on, you got in the car, paused for a moment and then slammed the door shut. I placed my hand on your right leg whilst starting the car and you squeezed my hand tight. I didn't want to let go.

We got to the bowling alley, the girls were on top of the world. Your mum got the kids out of the car.

"I will take the girls in, I will see you in there" said Misha's mum.

I turned my body to look at you and took your hands, as I have now.

"What's wrong baby, this is more than a migraine isn't it?" you sat there in silence. "I can't help you baby if you don't speak to me, baby…. ….".

"You know…..fine!, sit here I don't care, feel sorry for yourself, you will not ruin the kids day, take a minute then come in, and at least try and paint a smile on your face".

I slammed the door so hard behind me you didn't even flinch.

"Ahhhh……..Yes I remember, I took a few minutes to compose myself. I was not really thinking straight. I got out the car and walked towards the building then I just carried on walking past and stood outside the pharmacy".

"What to get tablets, I thought you always carried some in your handbag?".

"If you wait a minute, I will tell you. I stood outside the pharmacy, I almost turned my self around, I went in and bought a pregnancy test."

"What you were pregnant?". He said.

"Well I did the test, so, yes. I had a feeling for months, I missed my periods, but amongst the stress and by the time I realised, I was too scared to find out. In case it all happens again like the first pregnancy.

So many thoughts running through my mind; how would I cope, the stress, the worry, not sleeping and eating, I couldn't go through the next 4 months in fear of what may happen. I will never get over losing Kris, I'm just not in the best frame of mind."

"I can't believe it, so much to process, how far gone?".

"5 months!" He shouted.

"5 months, you are barely showing, and you've lost so much weight. Oh baby why didn't you tell me, we could have got through this together. I could have supported you, or even seen someone to help".

"I'm sorry" said Misha. "I haven't been having migraines, I've just been struggling, I didn't know how to handle the situation. I love the girls with all my heart, but there's a part of me which hurts when I watch them play and sleep and he just isn't there when he's supposed to be, that's why I have been so distant. The grief had consumed me. I wasn't a very supportive wife to you either, when you must be feeling the same.

"I came inside the bowling alley and you had already started to play, I went to the bathroom and took the test and it was positive. I put the test in my handbag and came to join you".

"It's starting to come back to me in pieces now, will you continue?" (So the husband began).

The girls were starving and your mum was lagging, the girls were nagging me all morning for burgers and fries so that's what they got.

We got in the car and just like your mum you both nodded off, I drove us to the drive in. I ordered the girls their food and gave them the food and began to drive off.

"Now be careful girls you don't drop it" within a few seconds.......

"Sorry dad, I dropped my burger'.

So I braked, took my belt off, reached round the back of the seat to pick up the burger.

It all happened so quick, the girls were screaming hysterically, we got hit by a lorry.

The next thing I remember was waking up outside the car, I assumed I had gone through the front windscreen. I struggled to get to my feet there was so much blood dribbling down my face from my head.

'What do you mean you assumed you had gone through the windscreen' I asked him.

There was so many firemen, police and paramedics at the scene, they were cutting away at the front of the car, of what was left of the wreckage.

"Please help them, get them out of the car, please, please" as I shouted and shook the paramedics.

"You have to get them out". No one was listening to me, they just seemed to shrug me off.

"Please listen, you need to get them out now, baby, wake up, wake up".

I fell to my knees, I gripped my hands tightly together to pray for you all, sobbing away. I got back up, stepped back and looked down to see my body lay in front of me. Before any emotions took over me, I felt a hand grab my right hand from behind. I slowly turned to my right and it was your mum, "how did you get...." Before I finished I looked to see her still in the car.

"But, but..." I couldn't even finish speaking, I was crying hysterically, but no one could hear me apart from your mum. I began to drown in the devastation, when I finally realised what had just happened.

It became apparent we did not make it through, I just hoped you and the girls would be okay. Your mum seemed to take it all in her stride.

They were cutting through the car and I could finally see them pulling the girls out from the back of the car, they were holding hands yet they were unconscious, they looked so helpless, I ran towards them to hold their hands.

As they were being placed in the ambulance they tore them apart from one another into separate ambulances. I jumped into the back of one of the ambulances before they shut the door and your mum went in the other.

They were attached to machines, left, right and centre, wires coming out from everywhere, they were covered in blood. We got to the hospital so quick, that I lost grip of their hands as they were rushed into theatre. It felt like hours as I sat in the corridor waiting, I kept my eye on the red light above the door as I paced up and down.

We knew you were strong, that's why we went with the girls, the fire brigade were still trying to free you.

I stood in front of the theatre doors, so many people were passing by behind me, and then the red light turned off. My tears stopped streaming, I felt as if my heart started to pound again. I held my head high and waited moments for the doctors to come out, then I felt two little hands reach for my hands as I saw the doctors come out repeatedly shaking their heads.

I was too scared to look down. I shut my eyes, turned to my left and Millie was there, I then turned to my right and it was Maya.

I bent down to hug them both in my arms as I sobbed. They were so brave. Millie, wiped away my tears from my face as Maya said 'don't cry dad, at least we are together now' they were brave beyond their years, and seemed to understand what was happening.

"Now we can go home daddy" Said Millie.

"It is beautiful, there is a castle, animals and our home, can we go now, can we?".

The girl's had seemed to have crossed over seeing glimpses of this world and the next, and didn't release they had to fight for their life, to them this was their future.

I stood up to see you had arrived at the hospital. Your mum looked at me and said you were in a coma, and there was a chance you may make it. I was happy that you may survive, but also sad that I would never be able to touch and hold you again.

As the doctors left your room, we all came in to say our goodbye, it was heart breaking and emotional, I can't describe the feeling in the pit of my stomach of how I felt knowing that I will never see your beautiful face again, and you would never see our precious girls. I couldn't do it, but I had to be strong for our girls. We all held hands and prayed together that you would wake up.

'More tears are shed over answered prayers than unanswered one'

-Mother Theresa.

The girls then whispered something in each of your ears, your mum kissed you on your forehead and I gripped your hand tightly. We could then hear a fading drum, gradually increasing in volume and a rainbow of light flashed inside the room and we were here in this beautiful cottage where we have been for weeks. This is our life.

I was saddened that I didn't have enough time to say anything to you and that you would be fighting this alone, but in spirit we were fighting for you.

Misha then spoke up after wiping away her trickling of tears 'when I heard the drums I thought I was dreaming, I wasn't, was I?

"No baby, you were drifting from one world to another. You had passed but couldn't cross over to us, you were stuck in the in-between, you struggled with departing, it took a while for you to reach us but you did. You had apparently passed hours after we left and since then you have been trying to find us. You had so many demons of your own to contend with, you didn't know if you were coming or going".

"Oh my God, it's all making sense to me now" Misha took a big gulp of her brandy.

"It felt like I was dreaming, but in fact it was a journey, I couldn't release myself from the life I lived to where we are now. I didn't want to let go. But I did and we are all now here together, I can't even imagine how the girls moved on so quickly".

"They had a glimpse of this life, experienced it for a brief few moments, to them it felt like a lifetime, their home. There was one other reason it was so simple for them" said my husband.

He paused for a few moments.

"Well....." Misha said sighing.

"On your journey towards us, you experienced so many moments, it's not just me and the girls whom have been living here...."

Misha interrupted, "what do you mean?".

"The girls met someone, who would also like to meet you, take a look". As he pointed towards the spider frame.

Misha started to choke up, her breathing became heavier, she dropped her glass on the floor, and lept to her feet. She gazed over to the spider frame and a small head with golden brown hair peered from around the back of the frame, wearing denim dungarees and red sneakers.

All three kids jumped from the climbing frame, landed on their feet and ran towards Misha, she dropped to the floor and squeezed Kris, rubbing his head with her right hand as her husband said with happy tears.

"Meet our son Kris".

"How I longed for this day, I can't believe it, all my kids finally together" she cried with tears of joy.

'A mother's love for her child is like nothing else in the world, it knows no aw, no pity, it dares all things and crushes down remorselessly all that stands in its path' (Agatha Christie).

It's not the end, it's the beginning......

Printed in Great Britain
by Amazon.co.uk, Ltd.,
Marston Gate.